S0-ARL-627

The Legend of the Hummingbird

A Tale from Puerto Rico

Retold by Michael Rose Ramirez
Illustrated by Margaret Sanfilippo

FOLKLORE CONSULTANT: BETTE BOSMA

Para mi abuelita, Carmen Bautista Millan Soto—M.R.R.
To Jesika—M.S.

Photograph/Illustration Credits © Anthony Mercieca/Photo Researchers:
p. 27; Cynthia A. Belcher: p. 28; © Porterfield/Chickering/Photo Researchers:
p. 29; Collection of Matthew S. and Hedy M. Santangelo/Knights of Columbus
Headquarters Museum, Library Collection: p. 30; Randy Wells/Tony Stone
Images: p. 31 top; © Suzanne L. Murphy/DDB Stock Photo: p. 31 bottom.

Text copyright © 1998 by Michael Rose Ramirez
Illustrations copyright © 1998 by Margaret Sanfilippo

All rights reserved.
No part of this publication may be reproduced, except in the case
of quotation for articles or reviews, or stored in any retrieval system,
or transmitted in any form or by any means, electronic, mechanical,
photocopying, recording, or otherwise, without written permission from
the publisher.

For information contact:
MONDO Publishing
980 Avenue of the Americas,
New York, NY 10018

Visit our web site at http://www.mondopub.com

Printed in Hong Kong
00 01 02 03 04 05   9 8 7 6 5 4 3 2

Designed by Allison Russo and Mina Greenstein
Production by The Kids at Our House

Library of Congress Cataloging-in-Publication Data
Ramirez, Michael Rose.
    The legend of the hummingbird : a tale from Puerto Rico / retold by
  Michael Rose Ramirez ; illustrated by Margaret Sanfilippo ; folklore
  consultant, Bette Bosma.
        p.   cm. — (Mondo folktales)
    Summary: A girl and boy from rival tribes have their love protected and
  immortalized when they are changed into a red flower and a hummingbird.
      ISBN 1-57255-232-8 (pbk : alk. paper). — ISBN 1-57255-234-4 (big book)
      [1. Folklore—Puerto Rico.   2. Hummingbirds—Folklore.]   I. Sanfilippo,
  Margaret, ill.   II. Title.   III. Series.
  PZ8.1.R129Le   1998
  398.2'089'9755—DC21   96-38004
                                                              CIP
                                                              AC

When I was a child, I loved to hear my grandmother's stories about the island of Puerto Rico. Many of her stories were about the exotic plants and animals that make Puerto Rico special. One of my favorite stories told why the hummingbird was created. As you read this story you, too, will learn the legend of this tiny bird.

Michael Rose Ramirez

PRONUNCIATION GUIDE

Taíno(s)   *tie-EE-no(s)*
Caribe(s)   *ka-REE-bay(s)*

High in the mountains lived the daughter of a chief. Her name was Alida, and her tribe was called the Taínos.

Alida's favorite place was the sparkling waterfall that tumbled into a small pool. All around the pool were rocks and tall trees. The trees kept Alida's special place hidden.

One day, while Alida was at the hidden pool, she was surprised by a visitor, a boy about her own age. The boy joined Alida on the rocks.

"My name is Taroo," the boy said. "I come to this place, too. I like to sit by the pool and pick fruit from the trees."

Alida and Taroo dipped their bare feet into the cool water, and they talked and talked. Taroo knew they were from different tribes, and after a while he told Alida he was a Caribe.

Alida was suddenly filled with fear. "But the Caribes are an enemy tribe of the Taínos!" she exclaimed.

Taroo tried to comfort her. "Yes, it is true," he said softly. "But I wish you no harm. I want only peace and friendship."

Taroo's words were sincere, and so Alida trusted him.

Soon Alida and Taroo became good friends. They met at the hidden pool whenever they could. They spent hours talking and laughing together.

Before long, their friendship turned into love. They hoped to marry.

The young couple tried to keep their love a secret. But one day someone saw them together and told Alida's father.

Alida was forbidden to go back to the pool, and her father immediately arranged for her to marry someone else.

Alida was filled with sadness.
One evening, as her wedding day
drew near, Alida called to the
stars. "Please help me," she cried.
"Don't let me marry a man I do
not love."

The stars heard Alida's plea. They knew of her love for Taroo and they wanted to help her. Quickly they changed Alida into a beautiful red flower.

Meanwhile, Taroo returned every day to their special place. He waited and waited. He did not know why Alida had stopped coming.

Then one night, the moon called down to Taroo and explained what had happened.

"Alida's father learned of your secret love and planned another marriage for her," the moon said gently. "But Alida asked the stars for help, and they changed her into a red flower."

Taroo was overjoyed. "Which flower?" he called to the stars. "Oh please, help me find her!"

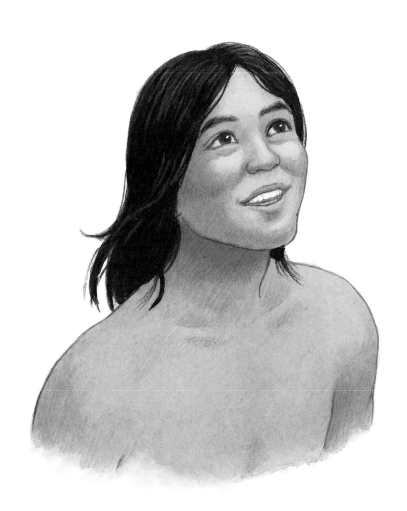

The stars heard Taroo's plea and
they wanted to help him, too.
Quickly they changed Taroo into
a tiny bird.

"Now you can fly," said the stars. "Find your love among the flowers."

And so the tiny bird flew off. As he did, his wings made a sweet humming sound that filled the night air.

The next day, the people discovered the tiny new bird. As fast as an arrow and as colorful as a jewel, Taroo the bird kissed each petal with his long bill, hoping to find the red flower that was Alida.

And the people loved the humming music the bird made with his wings. They decided to call this new bird the *hummingbird*.

From that day on, the hummingbird has hovered over many flowers, but it has always liked red ones best of all. The people say it is Taroo, still looking for his lost love, Alida.

P eople from many countries tell transformation tales in which humans are changed into animals or natural objects either to protect or punish them. *The Legend of the Hummingbird* is one of these tales from Puerto Rico.

Hummingbird hovering over a red flower.

Transformation tales are told around the world. In North America, Cheyenne Indians tell about a girl who saves her seven brothers from capture by taking them to the sky, where they become the Big Dipper. In England, Vietnam, and India, stories tell of a cruel prince who is changed into a frog. And in a German tale, a girl becomes a nightingale because she and a friend walked in a forbidden part of the forest.

NORTH

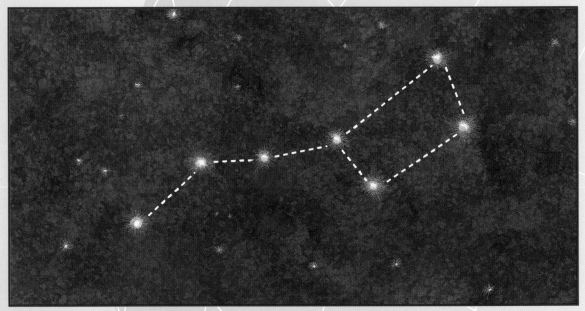

Spring sky, Northern Hemisphere

The Big Dipper is made up of seven stars.

The flag of Puerto Rico.

In *The Legend of the Hummingbird*, the artist shows how people of Puerto Rico long ago might have dressed to keep cool in the hot weather. Their small round huts were called bohíos *(bo-EE-os)*. The flowers and plants in the pictures still grow in Puerto Rico today, and the colors of Puerto Rico's flag are seen in the red flowers, blue sky, and white waterfalls.

The Taínos were the first people to meet Columbus when he landed in the New World. Spaniards and Africans settled on the island, and Puerto Ricans developed from the Taíno, African, and Spanish cultures. Most Puerto Ricans today speak Spanish. Many also speak English.

Puerto Rico is an island in the Caribbean Sea. The weather is warm all year. There are

Painting of Columbus landing in the New World.

Old and modern buildings in San Juan, the capital of Puerto Rico.

mountains, plains, beaches, and a rain forest. The cities have both old and modern buildings. Some people live and work in the cities. Others live in the country where they grow sugarcane, pineapples, and bananas.

Puerto Rican children like to play with dominoes and spinning tops. They enjoy many kinds of music including Afro-Caribbean *salsa*, African *bomba*, and Taíno *plena*. Some favorite snacks are coconut drinks and tropical fruits such as mangoes, guavas, and papayas.

Child enjoying a coconut drink.